For: Cindi,

Cherish the Playtime in every snow Storm !!

Scott J. Langteau

11·18·11

THE QUESTION

written by
Scott J. Langteau

illustrated by
Lidat Truong

"The Question"

Published by Shake the Moon Books.
www.shakethemoonbooks.com

ISBN - 978-0-615-53638-5

Cover design by Polina Hristova. Additional art by Steve Firchow.

Printed in China.

This book is printed in compliance with the
Consumer Products Safety Improvement Act (CPSIA)
Printed October 2011 Reference Number A49

Special Thanks To Vi Truong.

For
MiKayla, Kendra & Garrett

If it's
snowing
out now

as I lie
down to
sleep,

will it
snow
until
morning -

Will I **wake** to a window

of snow to the **Sky,**

leave me **snowbound** inside

with no **outsiders** told ?

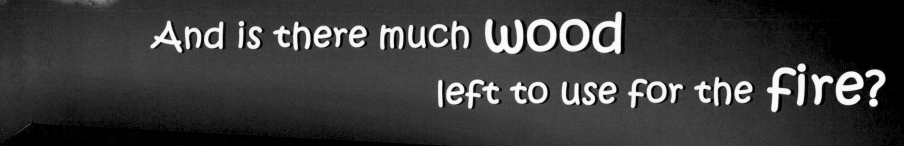

And is there much **wood** left to use for the **fire**?

If the
power
goes out

and our
flashlights won't **spark...**

...will we have any **candles**

to
light
up the
dark?

An **icy cold** floor

makes a great place to **Skate!**

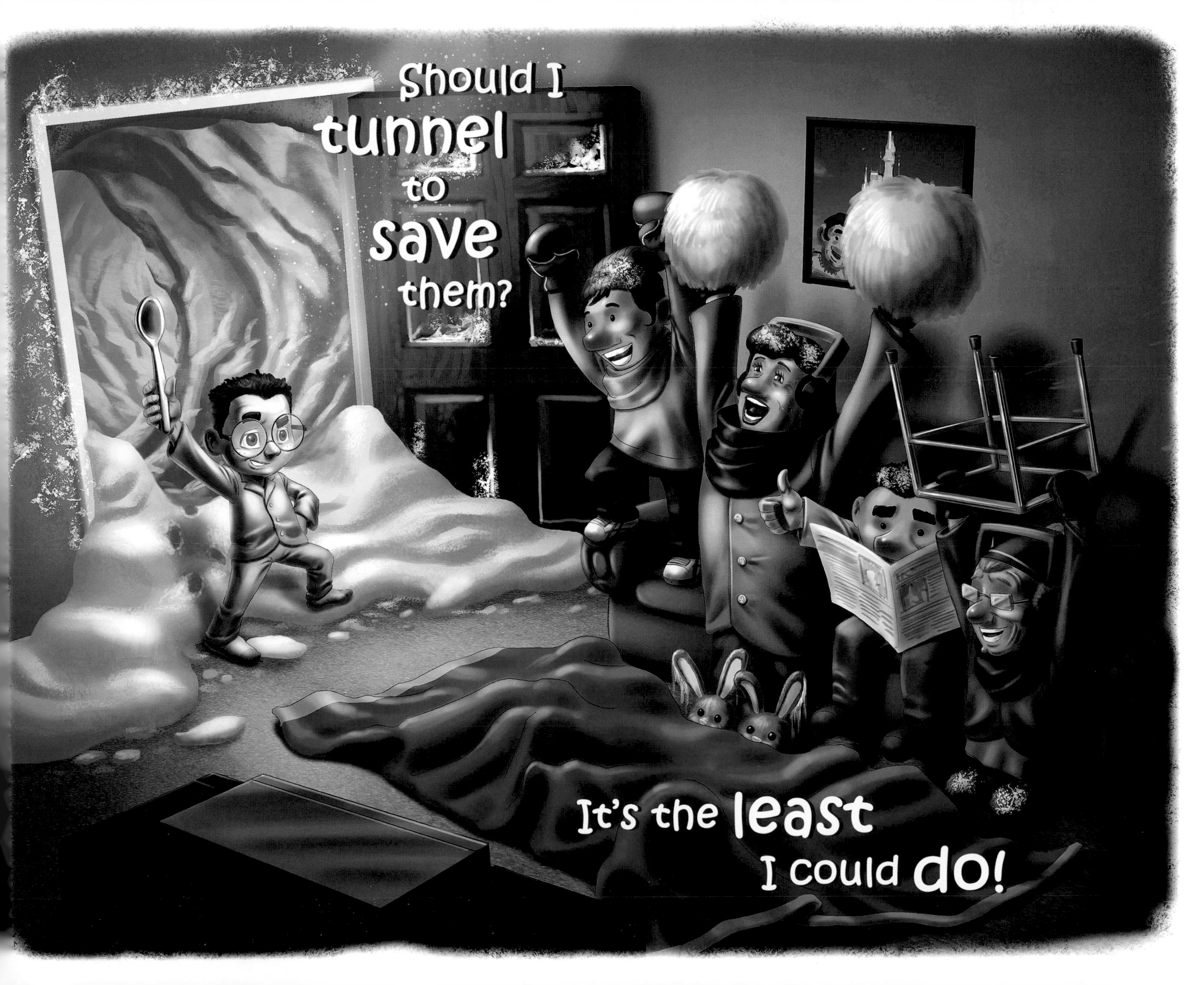

Should I tunnel to save them?

It's the least I could do!

If I'm **stuck** here 'til **spring**

as is **likely** the **case,**

As I get "Cabin Fever"

and quickly unwind,

will my
**teddy
bear**
"Boris"

come to
life
in my
mind?

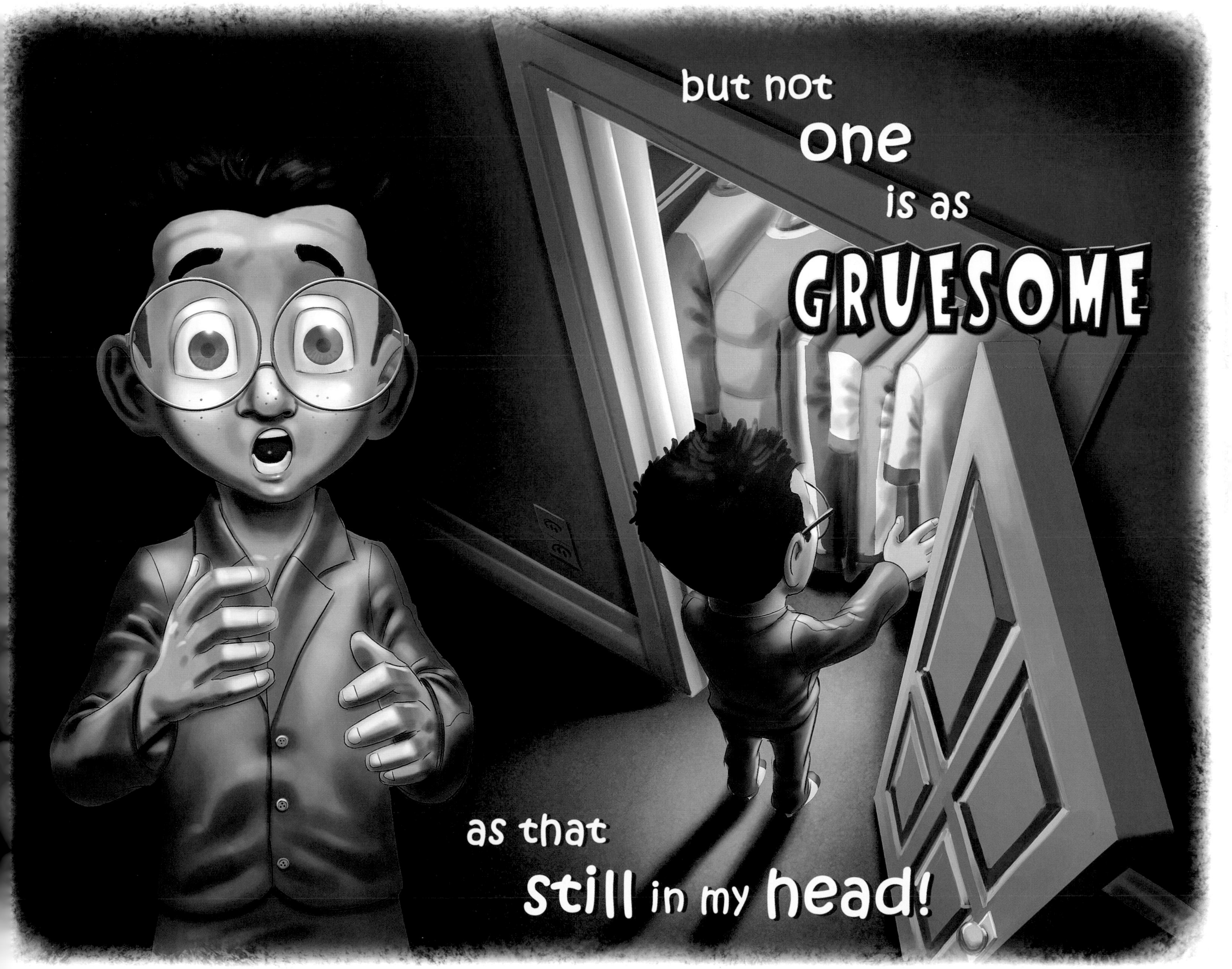

but not
one
is as
GRUESOME

as that
still in my head!

So I get myself **bundled** in all my warm **clothes,**

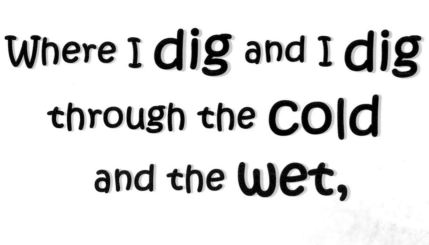

Where I **dig** and I **dig**
through the **cold**
and the **wet,**

and imagine
my **mother**

who'd be **MORE** than **UPSET!**

Then **burrowing** upwards I **bolt** towards the top,

and **burst** through the **surface**

having reached it **non-stop!**

Growing up in the snowy, "one traffic signal" (but thousands of cows) small town of Seymour Wisconsin, playtime came ready-made with Scott's 11 brothers and sisters. No fooling! Having fun then meant grabbing a sibling, heading outside and "imagining" a world around you.

That imagination brought Scott Degrees in Theater from the University of Wisconsin - Stevens Point and Villanova University in PA before landing him in Los Angeles where he has worked as an actor, writer, and producer for over 15 years. Best known for his work on the acclaimed Medal of Honor and Call of Duty game franchises, Scott has also worked for the likes of DreamWorks, the Jim Henson Company and Disney/Pixar.

Author of the award-winning title "Sofa Boy", Scott resides happily in North Hollywood CA. He secretly wishes that one day he'll wake up to find his neighborhood buried in snow too!

Scott J. Langteau

Growing up in Southern California, Lidat has been drawing since he was just a little kid watching animals at the zoo. A good portion of his childhood was spent engulfed in comic books and playing video games not unlike many other kids his age.

After finishing high school and spending a few years at UC Irvine, he decided it was time to take a shot at drawing for a living and enrolled at Art Center College of Design in Pasadena - from which he graduated in 2007.

Since then, Lidat has provided a wide variety of concept art, storyboards and illustrations for companies like Disney, Sony, and Vivendi Universal.

Lidat Truong

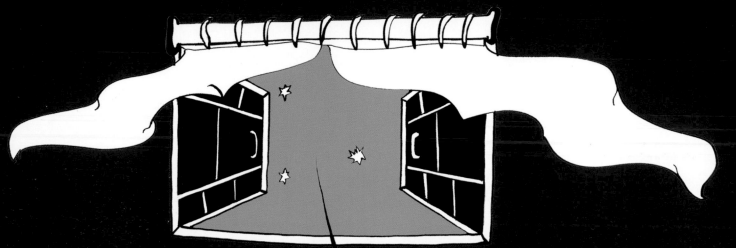

Original sketch
for
"The Question" -
(a poem)
written in April 1992.

- S. Langteau

For more information visit:
www.shakethemoonbooks.com

Shake the
Moon Books